JUST FOR
LAUGHS

Other Books by W.D. Ehrhart

Poetry:

To Those Who Have Gone Home Tired (Thunder's Mouth
Press; 1984)

The Outer Banks & Other Poems (Adastra Press; 1984)

The Samisdat Poems (Samisdat; 1980)

A Generation of Peace (New Voices; 1975)

Prose:

In the Shadow of Vietnam: Essays 1977-1991 (McFarland &
Co.; 1991)

Passing Time: Memoir of a Vietnam Veteran Against the War
(McFarland & Co.; 1989)

Going Back: An Ex-Marine Returns to Vietnam (McFarland
& Co.; 1987)

Vietnam-Perkasie: A Combat Marine Memoir (McFarland &
Co.; 1983)

As Editor:

Unaccustomed Mercy: Soldier Poets of the Vietnam War (Texas
Tech University Press; 1989)

Carrying the Darkness: The Poetry of the Vietnam War (Texas
Tech University Press; 1989)

Demilitarized Zones: Veterans After Vietnam, with Jan Barry
(East River Anthology; 1976)

JUST FOR LAUGHS

Poems by W.D. Ehrhart

Bill Ehrhart

Vietnam Generation Inc.
& Burning Cities Press

1990

VIETNAM GENERATION
Volume 2, Number 4

JUST FOR LAUGHS is published as a special issue of _Vietnam Generation_.

Vietnam Generation was founded in 1988 to promote and encourage interdisciplinary study of the Vietnam War era and the Vietnam War generation. The journal is published by Vietnam Generation, Inc., a nonprofit corporation devoted to promoting scholarship on recent history and contemporary issues.

All correspondence, including manuscript submissions, should be sent to Kali Tal, Editor, _Vietnam Generation_, 10301 Procter Street, Silver Spring, MD 20901. Style sheets may be ordered from the editor. If you wish your submission returned, please enclose SASE.

Subscriptions to _Vietnam Generation_ are $40. per year for individuals, and $75 per year for institutions. (Add $12 postage for subscriptions outside the US.) Single copies may be purchased at $12. per issue, or at $9 per issue for orders of over 10. All orders must be prepaid in US currency. Please notify us of change of address at least six weeks in advance; there is a charge for replacement of issues which are returned by the Post Office as undeliverable at the address shown. If claims for undelivered issues are made within six months of the publication date, we will replace the journal. We do not accept cancellations or provide refunds. _Vietnam Generation_ is published quarterly, in January, April, July, and October. Copies of the _Vietnam Generation Newsletter_ and access to the Vietnam Generation bibliographic database are included in the purchase price of the subscription.

ISSN: 1042-7597

Poems in this collection first appeared in the following publications:

The American Poetry Review: "Nicaragua Libre," "Unaccustomed Mercies," "What We're Buying," "Why I Don't Mind Rocking Leela to Sleep."
Colorado Review: "Chasing Locomotives," "Second Thoughts," "Starting Over."
The Connecticut Poetry Review: "America Enters the 1990s," "For Anne, Approaching Thirty-five," "Not Your Problem," "POW/MIA," "Twice Betrayed."
Cultural Critique: "Parade" (under the title "Parade Rest").
5 AM: "The Poet As Athlete."
The Kindred Spirit: "On the Right to Vote."
Modern Times: "The Next World War."
Painted Bride Quarterly: "Adoquinas," "Winter Bells."
Poetry East: "Lenin."
Poetry Wales: "In the Valley of the Shadow."
Samisdat: "Appearances," "The Beach Tree," "Letter from an Old Lover."
Stone Country: "The Ducks on Wissahickon Creek."
Studies in Education: "What You Gave Me."
The Tie That Binds, Papier-Maché Press: "Small Song for Daddy."
The Virginia Quarterly Review: "For Mrs. Na," "Just for Laughs," "Keeping My Distance," "Last Flight Out from the War Zone," "Water."
The Washington Post Magazine: "The Children of Hanoi," "Song for Leela, Bobby and Me."
Yarrow: "Who Did What to Whom."
Z Miscellaneous: "Some Other World."

Twelve of these poems were published by Adastra Press as *Winter Bells* (1988), a handset letterpressed chapbook. Additional poems have appeared in *Nasi Razgledi* (Yugoslavia), *Poetry Australia, Van Nghe Quan Doi* (Vietnam), and *Voices Israel,* as well as in the *1983 Anthology of Magazine Verse* (Monitor Books) 1985, *Only Morning in Her Shoes* (Utah State University Press), *Reclaiming the Pieces* (St. Lawrence University Press), *Unaccustomed Mercy* (Texas Tech University Press), *The Swarthmorean,* and *But Nhon Lua Viet* (U.S.A.).

My thanks to Donald P. Cassidy and Ralph J. Mills, Jr., and to the Pennsylvania Council on the Arts.

First Edition
Copyright ° W.D. Ehrhart 1990
Published by Vietnam Generation, Inc. & Burning Cities
Press, 10301 Procter Street, Silver Spring, MD 20901.

Cover painting, "Woman Nursing," (watercolor and
pencil), by Kalí Tal.

ISBN: 0-9628524-0-6

In Memory of
John Harry Ehrhart
December 7, 1918 — January 2nd, 1988
and
Evelyn Marie (Conti) Ehrhart
March 15th, 1920 — July 13th, 1990

Contents

IV.

V.

I.

Just for Laughs

When I was ten, I thought that I
would live forever, I could kill
whatever I pleased, I was all
that mattered. How else
can one explain the firecrackers
stuffed down throats of frogs and lit:
hop, hop, boom. A lot of laughs.

Once we found a plump snake
sunning itself beside the creek.
Sluggish in the early morning
chill, it only raised its head
and turned two diamond-black eyes
to see four small boys with sticks.

It didn't understand until we
started beating on its flanks
that we were dangerous
and it was trapped.
Our sticks were too light
and we too timid to inflict
anything but fury, so we
started throwing stones.

Small gashes ripped that snake's
fat thrashing sides until it
finally tired, though it couldn't
run and wouldn't die. It only
lay there heaving as the stones
fell faster—till a miracle
of birth began so strangely even
we were brought up short and stood
there for a moment dumbly watching:

out of those gashes crawled a dozen
baby watersnakes, a dozen more,
small wriggling slivers of their
mother's flesh; some were bleeding,
some had broken backs and dragged
limp tails sideways through the dust.

Premature, even the ones uninjured
that we carried home and put in jars
all died. But it didn't matter.
We had frogs and painted turtles,
salamanders, and a praying mantis.
Years later, I volunteered for war,
still oblivious to what I'd done,
or what I was about to do, or why.

In the Valley of the Shadow

Something made us bolt upright,
all zombie eyes, all ears and nerves.
Something out there in the dark
came breathing, stalking, waiting.

Our fathers, who bequeathed to us
this rotten patch of earth, this fate.
Satan. God. The government.
No matter: it was there and deadly.

All night we hunched in what we wore
like turtles, like the frightened kids
we were and were not anymore,
silent, lost, half-crazed, and deadly,

wanting women, girlfriends, mothers
to protect us, to descend in fire
on angels' wings, torch the darkness,
pluck us from this sad mistake.

No one came. Something stayed there
just beyond our range of vision,
just a shadow on our hearts,
and no one willing to admit

we'd rape our mothers, shoot our fathers,
overthrow the government and swear
our innocence to God or Satan
for a single drop of sun.

Something left us slack-jawed, staring
at our own reflections in the dark:
what we were, what we are, and will be.
Bent, we drag it with us like a cross.

Keeping My Distance

The ambush lasted only seconds:
caught in the open, mid-thought,
they fell like ducks, wings
useless, feathers fluttering.
Dead, the four men sprawled
beneath a squinting moon.

All of them were armed
for once: bodies with weapons—
a rare thing where women
carried rice for soldiers, children
threw grenades in jeeps, and even
elephants were strafed and counted.

I was elated, blood pumping
through my temples, nostrils flared:
one of those rifles was mine.
A custom ancient as the art of war.
Proof. What men need
to substitute for strength.

I kept that rifle
long enough to understand
I hope to God I never
have to find myself
in need of one again,
and one too close at hand.

Parade

New York City
May 7th, 1985

Ten years after the last rooftop
chopper out of Saigon.

Ten, fifteen, twenty years
too late for kids not twenty
years old and dead in ricefields;
brain-dead, soul-dead, half-dead
in wheelchairs. Even the unmarked
forever Absent Without Leave.

You'd think that any self-respecting
vet would give the middle finger
to the folks who thought of it
ten years and more too late—

yet there they were: the sad
survivors, balding, overweight
and full of beer, weeping, grateful
for their hour come round at last.

I saw one man in camouflaged utilities;
a boy, his son, dressed like dad;
both proudly marching.

How many wounded generations,
touched with fire, have offered up
their children to the gods of fire?
Even now, new flames are burning,
and the gods of fire call for more,
and the new recruits keep coming.

What fire will burn that small
boy marching with his father?
What parade will heal
his father's wounds?

POW/MIA

I.   In the jungle of years,
lost voices are calling. Long
are the memories,
bitterly long the waiting,
and the names of the missing and dead
wander
disembodied
through a green tangle
of rumors and lies,
gliding like shadows among vines.

II.   Somewhere, so the rumors go,
men still live in jungle prisons.
Somewhere in Hanoi, the true believers
know,
the bodies of four hundred servicemen
lie on slabs of cold
communist hate.

III.   Mothers, fathers,
        wives and lovers,
        sons and daughters,
        touch your empty fingers to your lips
        and rejoice
        in your sacrifice and pain:
        your loved ones' cause
        was noble,
        says the state.

IV.   In March of 1985, the wreckage
        of a plane was found in Laos.
        Little remained of the dead:
        rings, bone chips, burned
        bits of leather and cloth;
        for thirteen families,
        twenty years of hope
        and rumors
        turned acid on the soul
        by a single chance discovery.

V.   Our enemies are legion,
        says the state;
        let bugles blare
        and bang the drum slowly,
        bang the drum.

VI.   God forgive me, but I've seen
that triple-canopied green
nightmare of a jungle
where a man in a plane could go down
unseen, and never be found
by anyone.
Not ever.
There are facts,
and there are facts:
when the first missing man
walks alive out of that green tangle
of rumors and lies,
I shall lie
down silent as a jungle shadow,
and dream the sound of insects
gnawing bones.

Last Flight Out from the War Zone

for Bruce Weigl

A long flight back—I, too,
fear the flight more than anything—
and then we'll be humping the boonies again,
stalking the past for a sign.
Isn't it strange how it never ends?

I like your resolves—clear and neat
like a compass and map in articulate hands:
to get out of the South, forever;
never to kill yourself; to value
the moments of the modest present.
We have lost so much, you and I;
it is better to keep things simple.

Friend, we must cling to what little
the war didn't take; our voices,
the singular vision, that hard sleep
from which you jump
as if you've seen something.
You have. And I have.

So listen when I say this:
take care of your beautiful life,
and trust me. The long flight,
the long hump into the gathering night,
what do they matter?
We will walk point together.

For Mrs. Na

Cu Chi District
December 1985

I always told myself,
if I ever got the chance to go back,
I'd never say "I'm sorry"
to anyone. Christ,

those guys I saw on television once:
sitting in Hanoi, the cameras rolling,
crying, blubbering
all over the place. Sure,

I'm sorry. I never meant
to do the things I did.
But that was nearly twenty years ago:
enough's enough.

If I ever go back,
I always told myself,
I'll hold my head steady
and look them in the eye.

But here I am at last—
and here you are.
And you lost five sons in the war.
And you haven't any left.

And I'm staring at my hands
and eating tears,
trying to think of something else to say
besides "I'm sorry."

Twice Betrayed

for Nguyen Thi My Huong
Ho Chi Minh City
December 1985

Some American soldier
came to your mother for love,
or lust, a moment's respite from loneliness,
and you happened. Fourteen years later,
I meet you on the street at night
in the city that was once called Saigon,
and you are almost a woman,
barefooted, dressed in dirty clothes,
beautiful with your one shy dimple.

It doesn't really matter who won;
either way, you were always destined
to be one of the losers:
if he wasn't killed, your father left
for the place we used to call The World
years before the revolution's tanks
crushed the gates of the old regime forever.

Now we sit on a bench in a crowded park
burdened by history. It isn't easy
being here again after all these years.
I marvel at your serenity—but of course,
you can't possibly know who I am,
or how far I have come to be here.
You only know that I look like you,
that together we are outcasts.

And so we converse in gestures and signs
and the few words we can both understand,
and for now it almost seems enough
just to discover ways to make you smile.

But it isn't, and I have no way
to tell you that I cannot stay here
and I cannot take you with me.
I will tell my wife about you.
I will put your photograph on my desk.
I will dream you are my own daughter.
But none of that will matter
when you come here tomorrow
and I'm gone.

Second Thoughts

for Nguyen Van Hung

You watch with admiration as I roll
a cigarette from papers and tobacco.
Hanoi. The Rising Dragon. 1985.
You can't do what I can do
because it takes two hands

and you have only one, the other
lost years ago somewhere near Laos.
I roll another one for you. You smile,
then shrug, as if deformity from war
were just a minor inconvenience.

Together we discover what we share:
Hué City. Tet. 1968.
Sipping *lua moi*, we walk again
familiar ground when you were whole
and I was whole and everything around us

lay in ruins, dead or burning.
But not us. Not you or I. We're partners
in that ugly dance of men
who do the killing and the dying
and survive.

Now you run a factory; I teach and write.
You lost your arm, but have no
second thoughts about the war you fought.
I lost a piece of my humanity,
its absence heavy as a severed arm—

but there I go again; those second thoughts
I carry always like an empty sleeve
when you are happy just to share
a cigarette and *lua moi*, the simple joy
of being with an old friend.

Who Did What to Whom

Hue, Vietnam

Because this street was washed with fire,
because I nearly drowned in fire,
I have come here again to sift the ashes.

How did I ever find myself
stumbling through Asia
dropping lighted matches like a fool?
"Okay, fool, you want some trouble?"
And they lit me up but good.

I have walked this street each day
ever since; each day the fire startles,
boys beside me go down screaming
or in silence, rise like smoke,
and I can't find a reason
that doesn't leave me burning.

But there are no ashes here, nothing
I can touch. Just some buildings
I recall; just the ghosts of soldiers.
These people don't remember me.
Curious, they only smile and stare.

Whatever might have hurt me here
is far away in quiet rooms
pouring over maps and plotting fire.

II.

The Origins of Passion

I am eight years old and naked
in my mother's bedroom: lipsticks,
brushes, combs and stockings fragrant
with her blessing hands, the vanity
an altar, I her secret acolyte.
A white lace slip drapes carelessly
across a chair; I take it in my hands,
press my face too deeply in its folds,
lift my trembling arms and drop it
over me, aching with desire
I can't articulate or understand,
immersed in her, burning with loss.

In all the years to come, I will
make love to women smelling softly
of lavender and talc, blessing me
with hands adept at rituals I want
to share but don't know how or why:
lipsticks, brushes, combs and stockings.
I will beg my wife to leave
her slip on; I will press my face
between her breasts and thighs and buttocks
too deeply, burning
to immerse myself in what I love,
still inarticulate, uncomprehending.

Winter Bells

In the dark breath of February,
how your voice lightly rises
over clouds, cold rain, the first
flat gray of early dawn,
lifting me into another day.
Small miracle, such magic.

I almost died in February,
Hué City, 1968; and once I drove
non-stop for twenty-two hours
all the way to Coconut Grove
just to escape the cold,
such fear I have of cold

and the aching emptiness like cold;
February, so empty of dreams,
so like the life I labored through
season by slow season.
Who would have thought a single
voice could change the natural world

or my unnatural fear
of short days and a long life?
Woman with voice like a carillon
pealing the cold from my bones.

A Scientific Treatise for My Wife

The ancients thought the world is flat
and rides upon a turtle's back,
or that the planets, sun and stars
revolve around the earth in crystal spheres.

Thus they defined the universe
till Galileo burst simplicity
by gazing at the heavens with a glass,
confirming Kepler and Copernicus.

All hell broke loose,
churchmen apoplectic, and the renaissance,
and finally Newton to explain it all,
a scientific substitute for Adam's fall.

Not exactly simple, but it worked
till Einstein stumbled on some quirks
in Newton's logic, and explicable
at last evolved incomprehensible.

Not good enough, said Stephen Hawking,
who proceeded to apply his daunting
intellect to postulating ways
black holes disfigure time and space.

He's got a Cambridge Ph.D.;
he's looking for a unifying theory,
and he's covered acres with equations.
Amazing. Centuries of speculation.

Okay, I'm not a physicist.
But even geniuses can miss the obvious,
and I don't need a Ph.D. to know
the universe begins and ends with you.

For Anne, Approaching Thirty-five

Alone in the basement, sorting clothes,
I found that pair of panties I like
(the beige ones with the lacy waist).

I meant to put them in the washer—
but they felt so smooth, so soft, I
just stood there getting hard. Woman,

never mind the crows' feet and creeping slack.
For me, you'll always be sultry,
mysterious, ready for anything.

Why I Don't Mind Rocking Leela to Sleep

Sitting at night on the porch
with my daughter asleep in my arms,
I thought I heard a rifle shot—
that singular crack
with no past
and a future chiseled in stone.

It was only a car,
but the memory of bullets
shivered a cold hole tunneling
half the distance to dawn.

＊

Once, when I was a boy,
standing alone in my father's church
amid the rows of polished pews,
ponderous oak beams pushing
the darkened ceiling aloft, a Jesus
larger than life knocking softly
at the door to the heart
of the stained-glass window
lit by a distant streetlamp,
I heard a voice,
and I thought it was God.
It terrified me home to fitful sleep.

*

Strange god, to sing such a voice
in the heart of a small child.
But the world is a strange creation,
and now my own small child
cries out in her sleep,
and I wonder what she is dreaming
and what she has heard.

*

What hurts most
is the plodding sameness
of cruelty, a circular world
impervious to change,
the grinding erosion of hope
stripping the soul.
These days, it almost seems enough
just to accomplish the household chores
and still be ready for work.

*

What I want for my daughter
she shall never have:
a world without war, a life
untouched by bigotry or hate,
a mind free to carry a thought
up to the light of pure possibility.

She should be young forever.
I could hold her here in my arms
and offer her comfort,
a place to rest,
the illusion, at least, of shelter.
I don't want her
ever to be alone in a world
with the Gentle Shepherd
frozen in glass and the voice
of a pitiless, idiot god
chasing her down the years.

Some Other World

Was there ever a moment
more perfect than this?
The house all dark, the wind
at the windows, the warmth
of your body against my chest,
and you asleep in my arms.

I thought for awhile
you would never stop crying:
the knife-edged howl, the sucking gasp
for breath, the quivering lower lip—
but I'm learning what troubles
an infant's dreams can be soothed
with patience and time.

Once, before you were born,
I watched for a moment
an egret ascend from a pond
with the grace of a whisper.
And once I dreamed a man
with a rifle refused to take aim;
I awoke to a sadness
deeper than dreams.

And I'm wishing this moment
could last forever; I'm wishing
the things that trouble my dreams
could be kept outside like the wind.

III.

The Facts of Life

Winter, and a gray storm sea
behaved as if we didn't matter,
driving the main deck under water,
breaking over the flying bridge,
leaving the catwalks slick with ice.
Even our tanker seemed to ignore
its own despair, wallowing
steadily north like a floating brick.

For a night and a day we didn't eat
or sleep or change our filthy clothes,
staring into a sky the color of ash,
trying to will the weather to break,
even the old salts studying clouds,
reluctant to meet each other's gaze.
And the freezing rain blown horizontal,
sweeping the decks like shotgun blasts.

Bells down in the engineroom.
The slow finger of moving light
from the lightship off Columbia Bar
barely able to bore a hole
in the smothering darkness. Christ,
why did we ever come to sea?
Where are the whales and porpoises,
the thousand mermaids singing?

Then the ship turned east, Astoria,
the shelter of the river, still
invisible across that deadly patch
of turbulence, the criss-cross waves,
the shifting sandbars just beneath
the surface, tossing steel like cork,
and all of us in life preservers,
hatches battened, portholes battened.

Maybe we would make it over.
Maybe by tomorrow we'd be drinking
beer in bars in downtown Portland.
Maybe we would sail again. Or maybe
we would finally prove what any sailor
understands, the scientists be damned:
the earth is flat, you reach the edge,
fall off, and don't come back.

Letter from an Old Lover

After all these years, how strange
to find your letter in the mail.
The year I spent at sea, I stood for hours
on the fantail, leaning on the rail,
the gnawing ache like cancer
of the heart, the lights of California
luminescent in the darkness. Beyond
the lights, the dark shadows
of the coastal range. Beyond the mountains,
three thousand miles of darkened continent.
Then the pilot boat, the tugs, and bells
clanging in the engine room: half ahead, dead
slow; Long Beach, home port, perhaps a letter
this time.

Now, ten years later, here it is at last:
the missing letter, re-routed back and forth
across three thousand solitary dreams.
I'm married now, and you're a relic
from an old life that's long since past.
The letter lies unopened on my desk.
Alone, I sit and study the address,
the postmark, the flowing script.
I don't regret a moment—then or now.
I only wonder what you have to say
that couldn't have been said
long ago.

Love in an Evil Time

for Diana Bedell

There was a woman I knew.
There was a candle, an altar,
a window, soft curves and shadows.
Miracles stirred in her eyes:

that she could raise the dead;
that she could see through the darkness;
that I could fall into those eyes
and just keep falling forever.

I hadn't known the gun was loaded.
I hadn't known how far I was from home.
I didn't believe I deserved it.
I didn't know what to do.

Trees lifted the moon into the sky.
In the moonlight, ordinary men
tore flesh from a broken corpse;
they grinned like dogs at a banquet.

No one explained this to me.
The woman sat beside me
singing of tea and oranges.
I wanted to slide into her.

I wanted her to kiss my wounds.
She kissed me on the mouth,
then blew the candle out
and left without another word.

Somebody cried, but it wasn't me.
Somebody burned the trees and the moon.
Somebody died of a dirty needle.
The dogs left nothing but bones.

Starting Over

for Nguyen Thi Kim Thanh

You were eight years old when you hunched
in your home during Tet. Saigon. Gunfire
rattled the ritual table your father set
with incense, moon cakes, and photographs
of the family's ancestors, praying for their
spirits' safe return. The family all together,
fireworks and dragons were to celebrate
the New Year. But not that year,

nor any year to come. The war persisted
like a slow tide advancing and receding
and advancing yet again, the old regime
rotting like a corpse from the inside out,
the end, when it came, coming swiftly, the cost
of privilege, even modest privilege, steep.
You left because a stranger in a foreign land
seemed better than a stranger in your own.

World enough and time now for second thoughts,
alone, you struggle with a second tongue,
snow and ice of Boston, and the effort to create
a life from nothing you remember but the smell
of incense and your father's prayers at Tet
when Tet meant time for calling family spirits
safely home, the family all together, each heart
renewed, forgiving, full of hope.

What You Gave Me

for Jeff Apple

Even when we were nine,
you were what I wanted to be:
the brave one plunging into the creek's
green slime barefooted, catching snakes
barehanded with a careless skill
and courage I could only dream of.

I swam in your wake,
sat on the bench while you became
State Champ, watched you lift my weight
in solid iron as the years passed.

You bought the motorcycle,
always waited for the girls to call,
and the phone was always ringing.
I got the grades, but who puts grades
in the family den like trophies?
What teenaged girl ever yearned
to be kissed by a straight-A student?

Once, much later, we were twenty-two,
some girl you liked had dumped you.
We were sitting in your kitchen.
"I feel so blue," you said, "I wish
I knew a way to say it like you can."

I'd never realized you might envy me,
that being held back in school
had bothered you. Your silence
always seemed so strong,
not the cowed shyness of a boy
well-meaning grown-ups had convinced
that he was dumb.

Every time I get a student
who's a little slow with words,
I remember that you never seemed
to notice how I waded in the creek
with sneakers on, the snakes each time
somehow just barely out of reach,
that you knew but didn't care
I wet the bed till I was nearly twelve,

that kids who can't articulate the blues
are songbirds locked in small cages
alone in darkened rooms.

The Poet as Athlete

for Lou

One look at him induces adjectives:
gargantuan, Brobdingnagian, humongous;
what manatees might look like
if they put on clothes. Somewhere under
all that vast expanse like open ocean
must be something solid, but no imagination
could be vast enough to conjure even
flaccid muscles, bones like coral atolls
in that briny, rolling sea.

Against the tide of gravity, he struggles
to the podium like someone swimming,
takes a drink of water, and begins:
a poem about the powerful intoxication
of his first car, a poem about
the expectation of a first teenaged love,
a poem about a son he doesn't have.

Surely he must know what we are thinking.
Surely he must swim through every day
against a tide of gravity and ridicule,
but in a sure voice steady as the tides,
he draws us to the heart
of what we share.

Not one word about his own affliction.
Consider poetry, how good poems
offer us the world with eyes renewed.
Now see the swimmer I am watching:
all discipline, all muscle, lean and hard.

Water

A dry spring after an April
that promised better: funny, the way
the weather seems to be drier now
than what we always remember.
We draw the Delaware River down
to cover the difference, build a new
power plant, cover our pastures
with houses, wonder whatever
became of summer evenings
on porches with thunderstorms.
The radio says it may rain today
every day for a week, but the sky
gives up nothing but blank blue
space from here to the moon.
Men have walked on the moon,
but the salt line on the Delaware
inches its way north year by year.
We believe the earth will go on
giving forever, and we don't believe
what we can see with our own eyes:
dust devils, withering violets—all
we need is a little rain.
We turn on the radio, gaze
up at the sky, and wait.

The Ducks on Wissahickon Creek

It's never as simple as this, of course.
Most of the time, hard questions

gnaw at the brain like rats,
and it's hard to imagine a life

that isn't forever perplexing.
But today, with last night's snow

still undisturbed and slowly turning
wet and heavy under February sun,

a pair of mallards followed
by a pair of perfect wakes paddled

side by side through quiet water,
so sure of where they were going.

The Beech Tree

My neighbor leans across the fence
and gestures upward grandly, making
with his two arms a tiny human
imitation of a beech tree lifting
two hundred years of sprawling growth.
"Quite a tree you've got!" he says,
"By God, I wish I owned it."

But though it lives in my backyard,
this tree belongs to the squirrels
leaping branches just beyond my window.
"You'd like to catch us, but you can't,"
they seem to scold the tabby cat
that crouches daily with a patience
too dim to comprehend the squirrels
own this tree and will not fall.

It belongs to the robins that nested
last year in a high sheltered fork.

It belongs to the insects burrowing
beneath its aging bark like miners.

I'm just the janitor: raking leaves,
pruning limbs to keep them from collapsing
the garage roof next door or climbing
into bed beside my wife and me.

Possession is a curious thing:
some things are not for owning,
and I don't mind caring for a tree
that isn't mine. I take my pay
in April re-awakening and summer shade.
Just now, I'm watching snow
collecting in the upper branches,
waiting for the robins to come home.

The Heart of the Poem

Split the ribcage open
with a heavy-bladed knife,
a hatchet or an axe.
Be careful with an axe;
it can do more damage than you need.

Grasp the ribs and pry them back.
They won't want to give at first:
pull hard and steadily;
keep pulling till they snap.

Forget about the skin;
it'll tear when the ribs give way.

After that, it's easy:
push the other guts aside,
let your fingers dig until the heart
seats firmly in your palm
like a baseball or a grapefruit,
then jerk it out.

Get rid of it.
Sentiment's for suckers.
Give us poetry.

IV.

Appearances

The deceiver
slithers into its chair
and coils its heavy body
into a lump, its head raised
and weaving slowly over the desk,
the forked tongue darting
out of a kind of sleepy
half-smile, testing the air.
Another day.

Two signs hang on the wall:
"Right" and "Left."
The right sign hangs on the left;
the left one hangs on the right.
The mahogany desktop gleams
like the cold eyes of a snake.
Where are the mice?

A knock at the door:
an imperceptible flashing
of razored fangs.
"Come in," says the man
seated behind the desk,
"Tell me the nature of things."

On the Right to Vote

Believe in a raw wind scraping over the land.
Believe in the crackle of fire.
Believe me, nothing you have ever possessed
is yours. The makers of wind and fire
care nothing
for dreams that are not their own.
They care nothing for you—
not even enough to hate you.

You think I am lying.
I am not lying. I know
how swiftly the wind piles clouds into the sky,
how the fire suddenly rises,
how the rain falls into the open eyes of the dead,
how the dead lie silent, forever,
astonished.

Listen: a machinegun clacks
like rain on a tin roof;
someone is moaning in darkness.
It is your brother. It is your sister.
Even as you sleep, someone's finger twitches
on the trigger.

What We're Buying

Impossibly sprawled
as only the dead are capable of,
they have all been shot at close range:

six priests, their cook, her daughter.
The men have had their skulls bashed in,
their brains scooped out.

Like ice cream. Only the blessed rich
eat ice cream in El Salvador.
The poor eat silence, tears and dust.

The brains deliberately piled
beside these bodies are a warning:
fuck with how it is and die.

Ten years of war and taxes
and it still comes down to this:
Priests. Cooks. Children.

Not Your Problem

Avoid this place.

Here time travels in tiny circles
like the hands of a clock.

Here dust rises like smoke
until it rains;
then we lie down in mud
and dream of dust.

Here our children will never learn
to read or write; their teeth
will rot from their heads;
they will join the army, or die
like us beneath foreign bombs.

Here men with guns at night
make sleeping people in houses
disappear.

Here voters are branded with ink,
and those unmarked are found
days later in trash dumps.

Here being poor is a crime
unless we are also quiet;
almost everyone is poor,
and we can hear a bullet
being chambered a mile away.

We will change all this.

You won't want to be here
when we do.

Adoquinas

for the old man

I never thought I'd see the day
Somoza would be gone. But God
helps those who help themselves.
Somoza helped us, too.
Oh, yes. That's the best part.
After the earthquake, Somoza decreed
all the streets and roads
be paved with *adoquinas*. Somoza
owned the *adoquina* factory.
He made a fortune
selling *adoquinas* to himself.
So after we had finally
had enough, we tore the streets
and roads apart and used
Somoza's *adoquinas* for our barricades.
These we used to stop Somoza's
armored cars. We did this here,
in Masaya, in this very street.
Then our fighters killed Somoza's
Guardsmen with their homemade bombs.
We had nothing, but we won.
And I'll tell you why:
look at the belltower.
You think those holes are bulletholes,
but they're the wounds of Christ.
I've even seen them bleed.

Lenin

Managua, Nicaragua
July 1986

The remarkable thing
was not her age; my grandmother
bore a child at fifteen.

It was not her shyness,
as if I might not see that sweet
brown breast she offered to her son
if she didn't meet my gaze.

It wasn't the quiet incongruity
of dark rich hair framing
dark eyes hollow as an empty room,

nor the poverty of cardboard and tin
that was her home.

It was the cheap red bracelet
on her wrist, the profile of a man
dangling on a plastic disk.

I asked her who he was.

She didn't know.

Nicaragua Libre

for Flavio Galo

When they dragged me out of sleep
that night and took me to their prison,
I was eighteen. They kept me chained
for twenty days, and when I left my scrotum
and my fingernails were burnt and blistered.
I had organized a strike of public workers
and they wanted names.

I'd like to say they all stank fat
and jelly-soft with opulent corruption,
but some of them were lean and sharp
as steel blades. I'd like to say
they all laughed happy and content
with what they did to me,
but some of them had eyes that never
seemed to see enough and never laughed.

They should have killed me. I gave up
organizing strikes and started organizing
armed resistance. Call it revolution,
if you like; I call it freedom.

Let them try to take my country back again.

America Enters the 1990s

The lies lie,
greasy and cold,
thicker than old gravy.

But you're hungry.
You are still hungry.
You were born
all belly and mouth.

It's not your fault
saliva speckles your lips
and your white eyes bulge
at anything
even remotely edible.

So you tuck the past
under your chin,
imagine silver candelabras,
fine china, delicate wine,
lick the platter clean,
and reach for more.

Chasing Locomotives

Tonight I pull a plastic locomotive
while my daughter wobbles after it.
Just learning to walk, she careens
down the hall like a small
drunken sailor on a rolling deck,
a tiny comedy. How many times
I've missed the obvious:

a world full of children, each child
a world in itself.
How can anyone so misconstrue
duty, honor, country,
he could make himself believe
some other parent's child
worth the cost?

Leela stamps her feet and shrieks and
off we go again. I'm tired. I would like
to let myself enjoy my daughter's laughter;
I would like to make myself forget
that mutilated child in its mother's arms,
a house amid dry paddy fields
crushed by heavy guns—

but it's little enough
my daughter has to keep her
from a world full of men
like me
who can't imagine any world
except the one they think
belongs to them.

V.

Animal Instinct

Asleep on my lap, the cat
twitches from whiskers to tail,
ears shivering, haunches pumping
anticipation of antelope
grazing the broad savannah

of her dreams: she stalks, pounces,
sinks claws deep into muscled flanks,
teeth catching the soft throat
and tearing, a memory of blood
perfect in every detail.

And there on the edge of her dream
a small, stooped, cunning figure
stands erect in tall grass, dangling
a wildebeest femur in one hand,
eyes darting, seeking his chance,

the balance about to be altered
forever, the femur slowly rising
through centuries, into the future,
into the now, patiently waiting
to strike the final blow.

The Way Light Bends

A kind of blindness, that's what's needed now.
Better not to know. Better to notice
the way light bends through trees in winter dusk.

What, after all, does knowledge bring? Cold rage,
the magnitude of history, despair.
A kind of blindness, that's what's needed now

because it's hard enough to pay the bills.
So long as you can still appreciate
the way light bends through trees in winter dusk,

what's possible, what is, what can't be changed
is better left to dreamers, fools and God.
A kind of blindness, that's what's needed now,

the wisdom not to think about what waits
in dark holes beneath the earth. Marvel at
the way light bends through trees in winter dusk

and don't imagine how the light will bend
the way light bends through trees in winter dusk
and burst forever when the missiles fly.
A kind of blindness, that's what's needed now.

The Next World War

A man with his hand on a trigger
waits for a sign from the gods.

He stands. He moves.
He begins to dance.

He dances on flames.
He takes the flames in his hands,

into his lungs, his eyes
burning, his hair, on fire.

He lifts his burning arms
to the gods.

The Storm

Midnight, and a rain falls black,
October cold, the wind obstreperous,
stinging.
        You wait on the unlit
platform, soaked and shivering,
thinking the years at once
too far gone and far too many
to carry.
        At last, the last
train to anywhere comes
out of the darkness, your dark
wet coat too perfectly black
until the train is almost past:

the engineer brakes to a stop
far down the tracks.
The conductor opens the rear door,
motions for you to run.

But you are where you belong,
it is raining and cold,
and what is a world or a life
without principles?
        The engineer,
the conductor, are wrong.

You hold your ground. The conductor
signals the engineer, the train
hesitates,

      then moves on,

              leaving you

standing alone,
heart filled with obscenities
cold and black like the rain.

How I Live

for Leela
who gave me the first line

I bumped my head on the setting sun.
The night had only just begun
and I was dizzy already, reeling
like a drunk walking on the ceiling
of a world turned upside down.

A steady star burned above the town
I thought I lived in, but I couldn't
find it, and a voice said I shouldn't
even bother, what with the wind
rising, clouds piling, tide coming in.

What was I supposed to do?
Jump ship? Run amok in Fortescue?
Abandon mother, wife and daughter
to the lunatics and pimps? Slaughter
common sense and go to sleep?

I couldn't stop thinking of the sheep,
the wolves, pigs, rifles, missiles
and a diesel east of Barstow, whistle
howling through the empty desert night
as if it were a soul in headlong flight.

Maybe I was only dreaming
all the lies, the calculated scheming,
computating, calibrating. Maybe not.
It never seems to end, I thought,
the dizziness, the mocking darkness.

Then an owl swooped low, the starkness
of its beating wings against the air
too savage, too beautiful to care.
Then a stillness, and a man alone
calling: Is it here? Is this my home?

What Keeps Me Going

Pressed down by the weight
of despair, I could sit for hours
idly searching the ashes
from my cigarette, the darkness
of silos, the convoluted paths
we have followed into this morass
of disasters just waiting to happen,

but my daughter needs to sleep
and wants me near. She knows
nothing of my thoughts. Not one
missile mars her questioning
inspection of my eyes; she wants
only the assurance of my smile,
the familiar placed just so:

Brown Bear, Thumper Bunny, Clown.
These are the circumference
of her world. She sucks her thumb,
rubs her face hard against the mattress,
and begins again
the long night dreaming
darkness into light.

The Children of Hanoi

June 1990

There in that place the Americans bombed,
where the children were sent to the hills
away from their mothers and fathers,
taking their laughter with them,
leaving their city in darkness,

in the market among the bicycles,
baskets of spices and fruit,
beer and cigarettes, burlap bags
and people singing their words
in a language forty centuries old,

in a toystore cluttered with orange
inflatable fish and wind-up monkeys
and dolls: two identical warplanes,
flight leader and wingman,
"U.S. Air Force" stenciled on the sides.

And the children touch them without fear,
pick them up with their hands,
put them into the sky
and pretend they are flying,
nothing but light in their eyes.

Song for Leela, Bobby and Me

for Robert Ross

The day you flew to Tam Ky, I was green
with envy. Not that lifeless washed-out
green of sun-bleached dusty jungle utes.
I was rice shoot green, teenage green.
This wasn't going to be just one more
chickenscratch guerrilla fight:
farmers, women, boobytraps and snipers,
dead Marines, and not a Viet Cong in sight.
This was hardcore NVA, a regiment at least.
But someone had to stay behind,
man the bunker, plot the H&I.

I have friends who wonder why I can't
just let the past lie where it lies,
why I'm still so angry.
As if there's something wrong with me.
As if the life you might have lived
were just a fiction, just a dream.
As if those gold Nebraska dawns
were just as promising without you.
As if Nebraska soil can grow things
just as well without you.

Since you've been gone, they've taken boys
like you and me and killed them in Grenada,
Lebanon, the Persian Gulf, and Panama.
And yet I'm told I'm living in the past.
Maybe that's the trouble: we're a nation
with no sense of history, no sense at all.

I still have that photo of you
standing by the bunker door, smiling shyly,
rifle, helmet, cigarette, green uniform
you hadn't been there long enough to fade
somewhere in an album I don't have
to look at anymore. I already know
you just keep getting younger. In the middle
of this poem, my daughter woke up crying.
I lay down beside her, softly singing;
soon she drifted back to sleep.
But I kept singing anyway.
I wanted you to hear.